# How I Became A Big Brother

# How I Became A Big Brother

## DAVE MOORE

© 2008

Published by 1stWorld Publishing
1100 North 4th St. Fairfield, Iowa 52556
tel: 641-209-5000 • fax: 641-209-3001
web: www.1stworldpublishing.com

First Edition

LCCN: 2007941970

ISBN: 978-1-4218-9838-4
eBook ISBN: 978-1-4218-9839-1

Hi, I am Joshua.
I live in a house
with my mommy
and daddy who love
me very much.

This is the house
we live in with all
of our pets.

My mommy invites her friends over who have little boys and girls and we enjoy playing together.

Then one day, my mommy and daddy told me that I was going to get a little brother.

I really didn't know how I was going to get a brother because my mommy's belly wasn't growing.

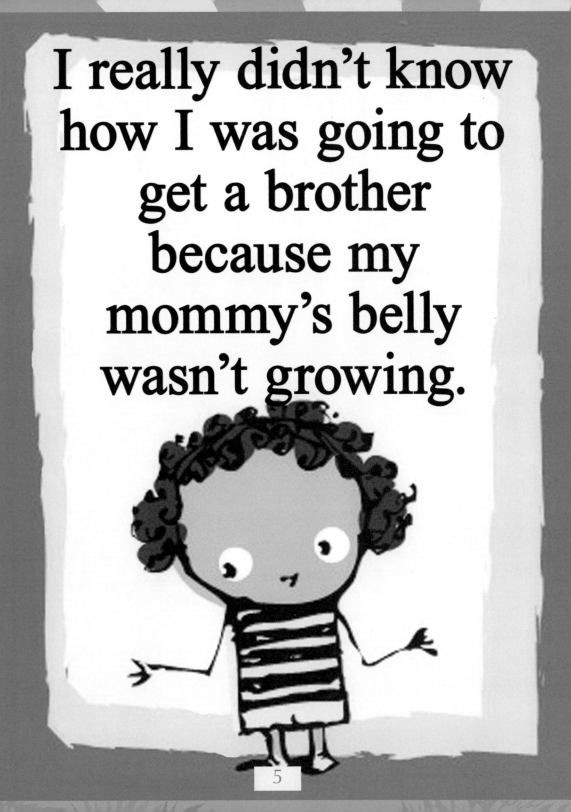

# Then my mommy and daddy told me about something called ADOPTION.

I didn't understand this but mommy and daddy said that adoption is when a child doesn't have a home and family to call their very own.

Because we have so much love to give, we are going to bring a little boy into our home and make him part of our family.

I was scared at first because I would have to share my toys.

Mommy and daddy said sharing is a good thing and sharing things with my brother would mean I have someone to play with.

Mommy and daddy
said they were taking
a big airplane a long
way from home to go
meet my little brother
where he is living.

The big day came
when mommy and
daddy packed their
suitcases and told
me that they were
going to be gone
for a little while.

After being gone for awhile, my mommy and daddy finally came home. We went to the airport to pick them up.

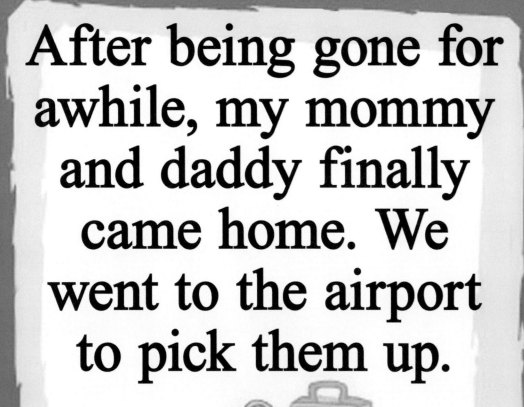

My mommy and daddy were very glad to see me and I was very glad to see them also.

I was excited to have mommy and daddy home, but even more excited when I saw my new brother.

He didn't look like me, my mommy, or my daddy. I asked my mommy and daddy how could he be my brother if he didn't look like any of us.

They again explained ADOPTION to me and said that with the help of many people around the world he would be my brother forever.

When we got home
I showed my new
brother all of my
toys and began to
share everything.

We all lived happily ever after and my new brother became my best friend ever!!!

See 1stWorld Books at:

www.1stWorldPublishing.com

See our classic collection at:

www.1stWorldLibrary.org

Lightning Source UK Ltd.
Milton Keynes UK
UKRC020321190520
363499UK00002B/6